Caroline Binch has illustrated children's books for Rosa Guy,
Rita Phillips Mitchell, Oralee Wachter and Grace Nichols as well as writing
and illustrating a number of her own titles. Her illustrations for
Hue Boy and *Down by the River* were shortlisted for the Kate Greenaway
Medal in 1993 and 1996, with *Hue Boy* going on to win the
Smarties Prize. Caroline is perhaps best known for illustrating
Mary Hoffman's internationally-acclaimed picture book *Amazing Grace*,
shortlisted for the Kate Greenaway Medal, which was followed by
Grace and Family, and the storybook *Starring Grace*, all published by
Frances Lincoln. Her other Frances Lincoln titles are *Petar's Song*,
written by Pratima Mitchell, *Since Dad Left*, winner of the
United Kingdom Book Award in 1998, *Christy's Dream* and *Silver Shoes*,
shortlisted for the Kate Greenaway Medal in 2002.

Quarto is the authority on a wide range of topics.

Quarto educates, entertains and enriches the lives of our readers—enthusiasts and lovers of hands-on living.

www.quartoknows.com

For Colin and Nina

Gregory Cool copyright © Frances Lincoln Limited 1994
Text and illustrations copyright © Caroline Binch 1994

First published in Great Britain in 1994 by
Frances Lincoln Children's Books

www.franceslincoln.com

First paperback edition 1997

A catalogue record of this book is available from the British Library.

ISBN 978-1-84780-258-3

Set in Plantin

Manufactured in Shenzhen, China RD112018

GREGORY
COOL

CAROLINE BINCH

F

FRANCES LINCOLN
CHILDREN'S BOOKS

"Gregory, you *just* like your photos," cried Granny. "It's your Granny got to kiss you at last, an' here's your Grandpa!"

"My, we so pleased to have you home," Grandpa said.

Sitting in the taxi from the airport, squashed tightly between his grandparents, Gregory wished he was back home with his mum and dad. Why did he have to come to Tobago?

The air was stifling and the strange smells disturbed him. Gregory shut his eyes. All of a sudden he felt very tired.

The taxi stopped outside
a very small house.
    "Do you really live here?"
asked Gregory. Granny and
Grandpa just laughed as they
took him inside and showed
him his room.
    The last he saw before he
fell asleep was a lizard
looking down at him
from the ceiling.

Gregory woke up next morning with just a sheet over him.
It was hot! Sun poured in through the open window.
There were no toys, no books, no carpet – not even
a proper door. Gregory scratched at his arm. Something
had bitten him during the night. Was he really expected
to stay here for four weeks?

In the kitchen, Granny was cooking breakfast and Grandpa sat at a small table with a boy Gregory hadn't seen before. This must be his cousin. His mum had told him about Lennox, and how he lived with Granny and Grandpa.

"Good morning, Gregory!" They all smiled at him.

"Come have some food, boy, then Lennox will show you around," said Granny.

Gregory sat down and looked at his breakfast plate.
Scrambled eggs – he could deal with that. But it
wasn't eggs . . . Gregory spluttered, and spat out
the salty stuff as politely as he could.

"Heh, you don't like your bake and buljol?"
said Grandpa. "It's just bread and saltfish."

"It's cool," said Gregory. "I'm just not hungry."
He drank a glass of fruit juice and followed Lennox
outside. Lennox was a year older than Gregory,
but much smaller.

"What do you do around here?" asked Gregory.
"Got a bike?"

Lennox grinned shyly at him. He had bare feet –
Gregory looked at them, then looked away quickly.

"Come, I'll show you the river," said Lennox.

The air was shimmering hot. Gregory sat down in the shade. "I'd rather stay here," he said. "It's cool."

"Well, I go feed the goats, then dip in the river," said Lennox, and off he ran.

Gregory watched him go. Didn't want to play with him anyway, he thought. How can he move so fast in this heat?

He stretched out flat, and dreamed of hamburgers. But supper that evening turned out to be meat so hot and spicy, he could only eat the rice on his plate.

The next day was worse – even hotter, more itchy insect
bites, and still nothing to do, not even TV to watch.
Gregory thought about going to feed the goats with
Lennox, but changed his mind. He wouldn't know how.
So instead he sat in the yard and played with his pocket
video game until Lennox came back.

He offered Lennox a game.

"Man, this is boss," laughed Lennox.

"You're letting them kill you," said Gregory. "Let me
show you." But Lennox jumped up and left, saying,
"You sure know it all, Gregory. You sure think you cool."

Granny appeared, carrying a big basket.

"Right now, children," she said, "Grandpa an' me is
taking you for a sea-bath."

"Wicked!" shouted Lennox, leaping around the yard.

"Cool," said Gregory politely. Cool was the last thing
he felt, but he wasn't going to say so. At least he might
get a fizzy drink and an ice-lolly at the beach.

The bus they caught was like an oven, crammed
with people. When they finally got there, the beach had
palm trees and sand, just like a travel poster. But there
wasn't anywhere to get ice-cream or chips – and Gregory
had missed out again on breakfast, so he was feeling
very hungry.

Lennox rushed off, cartwheeling along the sand.
Gregory sauntered after him. What was there
to get excited about?

The sea looked warm, blue and a bit rough.
Gregory was a good swimmer and he jumped into
the waves with a shout.

Suddenly, something he saw made him freeze. Sharks!
He started swimming for his life. When he reached
the shore he was spluttering and shaking with fright.

"Sharks? Oh no, Gregory, they're not sharks," said Granny comfortingly, "they're dolphins. Look see, the dolphin is our best sea-friend."

Grandpa was chuckling. Lennox fell about laughing. "You a fool, Gregory. You no cool."

Gregory stomped off. The sun blazed overhead, and
the sand was so hot under his bare feet that he had to run.
Two fishermen called him over, opened a coconut and
offered him a drink.

"Cool," said Gregory. "Thanks."

"Heh," one of them said, "what's your name?"

"Gregory," he told them. "I'm staying with my Granny and Grandpa."

"What you doin' with yourself, then? You been swimming?"

"Yeah," said Gregory. "I thought I saw some sharks, but they were just dolphins, so it was cool."

"Friendly sharks, heh! You got to watch them," they said, grinning. Gregory couldn't help smiling too.

One of the fishermen wrapped a big red fish in a leaf.

"Here, Gregory Cool, take this to your Granny. An' come out fishing with us soon."

Gregory was grinning
when he presented
his parcel to Granny.
    "My, what a lovely fish,
Gregory," said Granny,
giving him a hug.
"Tonight we have a big
fish-fry. Now sit down
and eat something, boy."

The picnic was fried chicken,
sweet bread, fruit and
biscuits. It tasted good.
By now, Gregory was
feeling thirsty again.
   "Got any coconut
to drink?" he asked.
   "Easy," said Lennox.

He went straight up a
coconut tree, no trouble
at all. It did look easy, but
when Gregory tried, the trunk
was far too tall and smooth for
him to climb.

Grandpa took one of the young
coconuts Lennox had brought down
and opened it with his machete. It was
full of juice.

"Mmm . . ." said Gregory, drinking it
in one gulp.

Suddenly he felt like swimming.

"Hey Lennox, I'm a shark," he said.

"Yeah!" shouted Lennox. "And I'm a
massive sting-ray."

The boys jumped into the water together.

Dusk fell. Back at Granny's house, Lennox took Gregory
up the hill to watch the moon rise. Gregory kicked off
his trainers. He wanted to be barefoot too.

Below them, the lights came on one by one in the small
wooden houses. People called to each other. Music played
on a radio and someone started to sing. Insects whirred,
dogs barked and a donkey brayed.

"Look at the candle-flies," said Lennox, and Gregory
noticed tiny lights moving all around them.

Gregory smiled to himself. Drinks from trees. Friendly sharks. A great new cousin. Maybe Tobago was going to be all right after all!

Granny called up from the house below, "Gregory! Lennox! Food ready."

"OK," said Gregory. "Cool Greg an' the Mighty Lennox, we comin'." Granny laughed and, as they raced down the track together, Lennox shouted, "Yes, you cool, Gregory – you really cool!"

MORE TITLES BY CAROLINE BINCH FROM FRANCES LINCOLN CHILDREN'S BOOK

Silver Shoes

Molly loves to dance, and she desperately wants
some silver shoes to wear to her first dance class. But her
mum says she has to wait and see if she likes the classes first.
Nearly all the other girls are wearing silver shoes,
even Molly's best friend!

Christy's Dream

Christy has wanted a pony for as long as he can remember.
Lots of other boys on the estate have their own horses, so now
Christy's saved up enough money no-one can stop him making
his dream come true. But what will his ma say when he
brings his new horse home?

Since Dad Left

Sid feels cross. He doesn't understand why his
mum and dad – Sandra and Mick – don't live together any more.
And when Sandra tells Sid she's arranged for him to spend the
day with Mick, he doesn't want to go. But Mick's offbeat
way of life turns out to be very different from most people's
and Sid can't help being drawn towards it...

Frances Lincoln titles are available from all good bookshops.
You can also buy books and find out more about your favourite titles,
authors and illustrators on our website: www.franceslincoln.com